D1515652

Jimi & Isaac 5a:
The Brain Injury

Phil Rink

Summary:

Jimi and Isaac are rock stars, epic heroes, intellectuals, and loving sons. They are wise and foolish, sublime and earthy. They are middle school boys, stumbling and shoving their way into manhood.

Isaac has always acted older than his age. So when Isaac's dad gets hurt, Isaac thinks he's ready to step in and take charge.

But maybe he's not ready.

Some things you're never ready for.

ISBN-13: 978-1501067594
ISBN-10: 1501067591

Look for us on the web.
Look for us at Amazon.com.
Get a copy for your Kindle or Kindle App.
Ask for us at your favorite bookstore.
Beg your friends to buy lots of our books.
Look for us on facebook.
Spread Jimi & Isaac throughout the land.

For Teachers and Helicopter Parents:
20,000 words.
Flesch Reading Ease: 93.6%.
Flesch-Kincaid Grade Level: 2.2.

Lots of ideas to discuss.
Not a book for small children.

Note from the Author:

I had very good help from medical doctors when I wrote this book, but it's a story about Isaac and his family, not a book about medicine. Some of the "facts" are wrong.

This is a hard, tough book about a hard, tough topic.

I wish I'd written it years ago. I wish I'd read it years ago. I'm sorry it took so long.

Chapter 1:
A Father-Son Project.

"Come on, Dad," I said. "Put the tape measure away!"

Dad just looked at me. "Measure twice, cut once," he said, looking back at the bracket for the solar panel.

"Twice, Dad," I said. "Not ten times. Let's get these things screwed down and hooked up!"

"Patience, my genius son," Dad said. He always calls me a genius when he thinks I'm acting like an idiot. "These panels are going to be on our roof for a long time. We might as well get them mounted straight."

"Alignment isn't that critical," I said. "Anything within ten degrees of south makes just as much power as pointing exactly south."

Dad ignored me. He was measuring twice again.

"You can't see these panels from the street, either," I said. "Maybe we could put some of my panels on the other side of the roof, too. Just to show off a little."

"Just to show off a lot, I think," Dad said, fiddling with the bracket.

He looked at me and smiled.

"These will be just fine," he said. "I think you've done enough showing off."

He was right about that. Once the press learned I invented the new chemical mixture that Weeds Solar used in the new panels, I got interviewed a lot. I was even on a TV show about smart kids. Apparently I'm the future.

Dr. Weeds's promotion and press campaign was crazy. They found all sorts of celebrities to talk about our solar panels. I guess they paid all sorts of celebrities to talk about our panels.

Dad said it was all a bunch of marketing crap. He had never thought that solar power was a good idea, in the big picture. But when Dr. Weeds got this famous string quartet to play a sonata on one of the TV commercials, Dad started looking at our roof. Suddenly the whole solar-power thing made sense to him. Mom said he was smitten with the viola player. Dad just smiled at that one.

After that, I told Dr. Weeds that he should make a TV commercial featuring drum players like me, except famous. He said you can't make money selling to drummers.

I grabbed the cordless screwdriver and walked over to my dad.

"Careful, son," he said. "Watch your step on the roof. If you start sliding, you won't stop."

I shuffled my feet a little. He was right. Sand came loose under my feet and made it pretty slippery.

"And leave the sand in the shingles," he said. "The sand keeps the ultraviolet component of the sunlight from breaking down the asphalt that holds the whole shingle together."

My dad is a chemistry professor. He's full of all kinds of useful information. But he gets really slow when he's doing something new. Sometimes he forgets he's working, and he just sits there and stares…"Cogitating," he calls it.

"OK, Isaac," he said. "Your turn. Put in one screw here…"

He pointed at the bracket near his foot.

"…And the final screw up there."

He pointed at the uphill end of the panel.

I already had the last three screws in my hand. Good thing we were almost done.

The cordless screwdriver buzzed until the first screw was almost tight, then rattled the last little bit until the screw was all the way tight.

"Great," Dad said.

He was looking right over my shoulder, like he didn't trust me.

Without moving my feet, I leaned uphill and reached over the top of the panel to put in the last screw. Pretty exciting, really.

Buzzzzzzzz. Raaaattttllllllle!

"Done!" I yelled, rocking back on my feet and putting my arms up.

The back of my right arm slammed Dad's face. He was way closer than I thought, still watching over my shoulder.

By the time I turned my head, all I could see were Dad's feet in the air as he fell off the edge of the roof. He was wearing his favorite suede work boots.

Chapter 2:
All Is Well?

The ladder was on the front of the house, so I had to run over the top of the roof to climb down. Running was stupid. I was going way too fast by the time I tried to stop. Luckily I was able to grab the top of the ladder before I went over the edge, and luckily Dad had tied the top of the ladder to a sewer vent that stuck through the roof.

When he did that, I teased him, too. "Stop worrying so much," I told him.

I slipped twice climbing down the ladder before I finally made myself slow down and made sure my feet hit the rungs. I was pretty out of control.

Then the front door was locked, and I had to run around the side of the house. Like a total idiot, I ran the wrong way and had to climb the fence to get into the backyard. If I'd run the other way, there was a gate.

"Mom!" I yelled as soon as I dropped into the backyard. "Mom! Dad fell off the roof!"

I didn't hear her answer, so I just kept going. I pounded my fist on the sliding glass back door as I ran by.

"Mom, get out here!"

Dad was lying flat out on the ground, facedown, in the grass. I mean his chest was down, but his face was toward the side. His feet were in the flower bed, and his head was inches from the concrete patio. That was a lucky miss, I thought.

I was pretty sure I wasn't supposed to move him, but I didn't know what else to do. He actually looked pretty comfortable, but he wasn't moving.

I got down on my hands and knees and put my face right down by his. I could see his breath moving the grass, and I pulled a dandelion flower out from under his nose. He wasn't allergic or anything, but it seemed like the flower should go.

But he wasn't moving.

"Mom!" I yelled again, rocking back onto my heels. "Mom, get out here!"

I put my face back down by Dad's. The grass was still moving by his mouth, and I cleaned out a few dead blades and the rest of the dandelion.

But he still wasn't moving. His eyes were a little bit open, so it looked like he was looking, but they weren't moving. That was a little spooky.

I put my hand on his shoulder.

"I'm going to go find Mom," I said. "Don't move!"

I didn't really think he was going to move, but I said it anyway.

The sliding door was unlocked, and I ran all the way through the house, looking in every room. I stopped yelling after I checked the bedrooms. Mom would have heard me by then. I still checked all the rooms, though. I didn't know what else to do. Mom wasn't in the house.

I ran back outside to check on Dad. Nothing had changed. I noticed one foot was kind of awkward-looking, so I started to move it to a more comfortable position. Then I figured he might have a broken leg, so I left it alone. I actually grabbed it and let go three times. It didn't look very comfortable.

The grass was still moving by his mouth, so I put my hand on his shoulder again and told him I was going to go find Mom. "Stay here," I told him.

The front door opened fine from the inside, so I made sure it wouldn't lock behind me and ran out into the street.

Mom was walking toward me, halfway down the street. She had a whole armload of iris plants she'd dug out of the neighbor's yard. They were taking out their flower gardens and putting in gravel beds, so they wouldn't have to water anymore.

"Mom!" I yelled, waving my arms at her. "Come quick."

"Come help me carry these, then," she yelled, "or just fix your own lunch."

"Mom!" I yelled. "Dad fell off the roof! Help me! Help me!"

She dropped the flowers right in the middle of the road and started running.

"Where is he?" she yelled as she ran past.

"In the backyard," I said, catching up. "I left the front door unlocked."

The front door bounced when she went through and it caught me in the shoulder, so Mom was already next to Dad when I got there. She put her face right in his face, too, just like I did.

"I didn't move him," I said.

"Isaac," she said, "go get my phone. We need to call 911. Hurry!"

Then she got back in Dad's face again.

We'd turned off our landline phones the week before, so the regular phone wasn't even on the wall where it used to be. It was just gone.

I didn't have a phone. Mom and Dad said I'd get a cell phone when I got my driver's license, and that wouldn't be for another two months.

Usually Mom's cell phone was in her purse, and usually her purse was on the kitchen counter where the old phone used to be, but the old phone wasn't there anymore and Mom's purse wasn't there either.

I looked in their bedroom, and their bathroom, and the living room, and the office. Nothing.

I looked in Mom's car in the garage. Nope.

I even looked in Dad's car, which was parked in the driveway. No purse, no phone.

But then I figured it out.

"Dad's phone is in his pocket," I yelled, running through the still-open back door.

Mom looked up. She hadn't moved. Dad hadn't moved. Mom never cries, but she was crying now.

She just looked at me, then looked down at Dad.

"I shouldn't move him," she said. "I can't move him. Just grab my phone."

"I can't find it," I said. "I looked everywhere."

She looked down at Dad again. Her shoulders were really low and round. She looked really small.

"My purse is with the flowers," she said. Her voice was smaller than her shoulders. "I had to pay for the flowers."

I was gone before she was done talking, but by the time I got to the middle of the street, the flowers were scattered everywhere. A car had driven down the street and run over the pile. I grabbed her purse and opened it up. Her phone was wrecked. Completely shattered.

Mom looked up with big, wet eyes when I got back. Dad was sitting next to her on the grass.

"Hey, son," he said, "nice purse."

Chapter 3:
Chaos.

"I'm fine," Dad said, dropping carefully onto the sofa. "Just let me sit for a minute."

"You're not fine," Mom yelled, right into his face. "You fell off the roof, and you were unconscious. You need to go to the doctor."

Dad just looked at her and smiled a little.

"I'm fine," he repeated. "I'll be sore tomorrow, though. I think I bruised a couple of ribs."

"At least put some ice on that bump," Mom said. "Isaac, grab a bag of frozen peas."

Our family has always used frozen peas as an ice pack. They work really well, because the little frozen peas don't have any sharp edges that hurt on your bump. You can push the bag right up against the damage. The key is to not eat the peas after you use them as an icepack. Thawing them and freezing them again makes them mushy.

Dad took the bag and held it against his head over his left ear. "This is cold," he said.

"Duh," I said. "That's kind of the point."

I gave him a little pillow, and he propped that between the bag and his shoulder.

"Better," he said.

Mom stood in front of him with her arms crossed.

"I don't like it," she said. She was making her disapproving face, too. She makes that face a lot, so we don't pay much attention to it. Sometimes we make the face back at her. That really makes her mad.

Dad just curled a little smile.

"I'm fine," he said. "It's a single-story house. Good thing we didn't buy the split-level."

That made Mom laugh a little, but she exhibited good control and got her disapproving face back right away.

"You watch him, Isaac," she said. "I'm going to try and save some of my flowers."

I nodded and sat in the easy chair next to the sofa.

"Don't leave his side," she said, opening the front door. "Not for a second."

I gave her the thumbs-up. She stared at Dad until he gave her the thumbs-up, too.

Then she left.

By the time Mom got back, Dad was watching a preseason football game on the TV, and I was reading a gardening magazine. I've always hated gardening, but there weren't any good magazines in the living room.

"You're good?" Mom asked. She had a whole armload of iris plants.

Once we both nodded, she started for the backyard.

"I think I can save most of these if I get them in the ground. Isaac, get more ice for your father, please."

I took the bag of peas from Dad and switched it out with a second bag from the freezer. I put the warmed-up peas next to the meat in the freezer to refreeze, so they wouldn't get mixed up with the food peas.

Dad took the new bag and held it against his left side. The lump was getting pretty big.

"That looks like it hurts," I said.

"Stupidity should hurt," Dad said. "I didn't need to crowd you like that, and I should have been more stable with my feet."

"I'm sorry I knocked into you," I said. "I should have waited to celebrate. I just got too excited."

"Looks like we both learned something today," Dad said. "Gravity is a good teacher."

"When Mom comes back, I'll go get the tools off the roof and take the ladder down," I said.

Dad just smiled.

"Tomorrow's soon enough," he said. "We've had enough fun for today."

Dad watched the game, and I read a magazine on decorating. The article said earth tones were making a comeback. Whoa. Exciting stuff.

Finally, Mom finished with the flowers and came in from the backyard.

She went straight into the kitchen. I could hear her washing her hands.

"Peanut butter and jelly or tuna salad?" she yelled.

"PBJ!" I yelled back. Then I looked at Dad.

He looked back at me. His left eye was black. The pupil took up his whole eye.

"Stack!" he said. His face got a little confused.

"Mix!" Now he looked pretty scared.

"Mom!" I yelled. I heard her drop something metal into the kitchen sink. She came around the corner into the living room.

She looked at me, then we both looked at Dad. His face was all twisted up, and his left eye looked like a hole.

"Numbers!" he said. "Yell numbers!"

Then his head dropped.

Chapter 4:
At the Hospital.

The paramedics were at the house and gone in an instant. They took Dad with them.

It was weird, too. It was real noisy while they were around, with radio talk and bags of medical gear getting ripped open and a huge metal cart they put Dad on and tackle boxes full of medical stuff. But in my head, it was quiet. I found a chair at the breakfast table and sat and watched. It seemed all blurry and quiet and far away.

The hospital was at the university where Mom and Dad teach. Mom and I could have walked there, but instead we jumped into Dad's car to follow the paramedics. Mom had to run back inside and grab her purse. When she got back to the car, she handed me Dad's phone.

"Call Jimi's house," she said. "Tell them what happened and ask them to come get you at the emergency room."

"No way," I said. "I'm staying with Dad! I'm staying with you!"

"No!" Mom yelled. I mean really, really yelled. Not like a normal mom yell at all.

"No!" she said again, quieter. "No. You'll stay at Jimi's tonight. Tomorrow…tomorrow we'll see."

She looked at me and started the car.

"Please, honey."

I dialed the phone.

Jimi's mom and dad weren't home. Jimi and his sister, Janis, could come get me now, or his parents would be home in an hour, then they could come. Janis had been driving for years. Mom and Dad considered her unnaturally reliable.

Mom was listening.

"Parents," she mouthed.

"Mom says 'rents," I said.

"Cool," said Jimi. "We'll be there as soon as we can."

"Thanks, Jimi," I said. "I gotta go."

"Wait!" Jimi said. I could hear his sister in the background. Her voice is pretty…distinctive.

"What else do you need?" Jimi asked. "Food, clothes, stuff like that?"

Mom was listening. She just shrugged her shoulders. It looked like she was going to cry again, but she was driving and there was no way she was going to stop.

"We got nuthin," I said. "We skipped lunch and…I think we left the house unlocked."

"I'll get your house," Jimi said. "I've still got a key. We'll be at the hospital as soon as Mom and Dad get home. Janis is calling them on her phone now."

"Jimi's a good friend," I told Mom after I hung up. "He knows just what to do."

Then I started to cry. I couldn't stop. It just kept coming.

The emergency room entrance to the hospital was crazy. There were people everywhere. Most of them didn't look very sick. Mom parked in one of the emergency spots right out front, and we went in.

She gave me the car keys. "Have Janis move the car, please," she said.

I could have reparked the car. I'd moved ours hundreds of time and would get my learner's permit in just a few months, but I saw her point. Plus, no way I was going to argue with Mom any more today. She was hanging on by a thread, I think.

Mom moved pretty fast. We pushed right through the crowd up to the desk, and she said something to the lady there. The lady pointed at some side doors that opened automatically once we got to them, and we walked straight through to another long desk. Mom said something to a guy sitting there.

He grabbed a clipboard and took us into another small room. There weren't any outside windows, and the walls were painted a pale green. I guess they hadn't heard about the earth tones. It wasn't like a hospital room, either. There were just a bunch of chairs and a few little tables. He and Mom sat next to each other, and he wrote and then Mom wrote and she showed him some wallet papers and her credit card and he wrote some more. I just watched. There wasn't anywhere on the forms for the son to sign.

Then he stood up and left.

"I'm going to go see Dad," Mom said. "You need to wait here."

"No way," I said, but I knew.

Mom just waited.

"OK," I said.

And she left.

I sat down.

When Jimi's mom came in the room, I started crying again. She came and sat right beside me and held me and kissed my forehead while I cried and cried. I felt like an idiot. It was embarrassing. Finally it stopped.

"I'm sorry," I said.

"Don't be," she said. I knew she would say that.

Jimi and Janis came over and hugged me.

Jimi's dad gave me a little hug, too. Then he went and sat down. Jimi's dad hates crowds and strangers. I'm sure it was really hard for him to be at the hospital. It was probably killing him.

Everyone told me how sorry they were, but nobody asked how Dad was. I didn't know, anyway.

I gave Janis the car keys, and she left to move the car. Then we all just sat. Jimi's mom held my hand. That was pretty nice. It wasn't stupid at all.

Finally, Mom came back into the room. She and Jimi's mom hugged and cried and hugged.

Jimi's mom waved at Jimi's dad, and the three of them stepped out into the hall.

"Talking about Dad," I said.

"Probably," Jimi said, "or about you."

"Yeah," I said. "Probably both."

I guess Janis came back with the car keys, because the four of them came back into the room and Mom dropped the keys in her purse.

Jimi reached under his chair for a plastic grocery bag.

"I grabbed you some clothes," he said, handing Mom the bag. "Isaac's are in our car."

Mom opened the bag and pulled out a white sundress, with huge yellow and black sunflowers on it. Then she laughed a little.

Jimi's mom grabbed the sundress and put it back in the bag.

"I'll be back later," she told Mom. "Slacks, jeans…?"

"Jeans would be great," Mom said, "and some T-shirts, please. And a toothbrush."

Jimi's mom gave Jimi a little pretend glare. "I'll take care of it," she said.

Jimi just shrugged, then he sat up straight.

"We forgot the food!" he said. "I left the sandwiches on the table!"

Mom walked over and gave Jimi a big hug.

"They'll feed me here," she said. "Isaac will eat whatever you made."

"Then we'll make more," Jimi's dad said.

I like Jimi's dad a lot.

Chapter 5:
Visiting Hours.

"Did you sleep OK? Mom asked.

She didn't look like she did. Her hair was on one side of her head. She looked old, too.

"Yeah, fine," I said. "We played some music last night, but after the first three songs, I just put the drums away and listened. Jimi's really getting good on the saxophone, Mom. He and his dad just go back and forth —really tight. Guitar and sax are almost the same instrument, I think."

Mom just sighed and patted the back of my hand.

"Can we go see Dad now?" I asked.

"We can," she said. "I want you to be prepared, but I don't know what to tell you. It's pretty awful."

"Like blood and stuff?"

"No, Isaac, not blood," she said. "Just…your dad is pretty sick, and they're using some aggressive treatments to make him better. It's not pretty. It's ugly, in fact. I just want…"

I waited. She just looked at her hands.

I've never really had to help my mom. She likes to do things herself. Now I wanted to help her, but I couldn't. I didn't even know where to start.

"Hey!" I said. "We should call Dad's brother. Uncle Bob is a doctor or something, right?"

"That's a great idea, Isaac," she said, smiling. It was a pretty good smile, in fact.

"I called him last night," she said. "He'll fly in today, and we'll see him this evening."

"It was such a great idea—" I said.

"—we both had it," she finished. She was still smiling.

Then she stopped smiling.

"Just don't be scared, Isaac," she said. "He's still your dad."

We had to put on gowns and masks to go into where Dad was. We had to pretend we were doctors. Then we needed to put hand sanitizer on. The sanitizer made my hands wet and cold before it dried away. The nurse said to make sure it got everything wet, even between my fingers and under my fingernails.

Right after we went through the door to Dad's room, I could see him lying on a bed, even though it was pretty dark. The bed was smaller than a grown-up bed, but bigger than a kid's bed, and it was higher off the floor, too. The back was tilted up so Dad could watch TV.

I stayed right by the door for a minute. There were little machines on both sides of the bed, and each one had blinking lights and knobs. There was even one of those machines drawing the heartbeat signal and a beep every time his heart beat.

There was a noise that sounded a little like a drum sound. It was a simple rhythm, though. Just a *wishhh-click*. Like a brush rub on the snare and then a little rim tap. Really slow, too.

There were three clear plastic bags hanging from a stand on one side of the bed. They were all connected together, and then one clear plastic tube ran down and under the sheets. That probably went to a needle stuck into Dad somewhere.

Under the bed, there was a clear plastic bag that was about half-full of pink grapefruit juice. It looked gross. I don't think the juice was medicine.

I couldn't see Dad's face. There was a bunch of stuff on his chest—more plastic boxes and tubes and hoses.

Mom walked right over to the side of the bed. There was a nurse or a doctor on the other side, looking at a machine and playing with the knobs a little. He didn't even look at me, but Mom caught my eye and waved me over.

Mom walked toward me and grabbed my hand as I reached the foot of the bed.

"He's still your dad," she said. "Remember that."

I looked at her face. She was looking right at my eyes, which was a little difficult because I was taller than her.

I didn't know what answer she wanted. Of course he was still my dad. My dad with a big bump on his head.

"'K," I said.

She didn't let go of my hand, but she turned and walked up to the head of the bed. I stayed right with her, in case she needed me to hold her up or something.

She pushed up as far into the equipment as she could, then she turned and pulled me tight against her. I looked at her face again. She was staring straight at me. Then she squeezed my arm and looked down at Dad. I looked, too.

It wasn't my dad. There was some sort of mistake.

Dad was never a thin, athletic kind of guy, but this guy's face was fat. Even if he had wanted to, he couldn't have opened his eyes because he had such a fat face, and there was greasy stuff oozing out through his eyelashes. He had a terrible blotchy haircut, and the whole left side of his head was purple, edge of his fat left eye. The rest of his fa yellow, with red smudges.

There was a clear plastic tube taped to that went right up his nose, and he needed

His lips had some of the greasy eye goo on them, too, and they were taped around a plastic hose that was stuck in his mouth. There were smaller hoses running into the big mouth hose. There were hoses everywhere.

This guy was a mess. He wasn't my dad. Dad just had a bump on his head and something wrong with his eye.

Suddenly I couldn't stand up.

Mom and the medical guy got me to a chair and told me to put my head between my knees and just sit for a minute.

Mom was crying.

Chapter 6:
Time Alone.

Uncle Bob picked me up from Jimi's house right before dinner.

"Let's go get a pizza," he said.

I felt bad for Jimi's mom, because she cooked a lasagna especially for me, but hopefully Jimi enjoyed the nonhealthy food. Usually they would have beans with sprouts or something with tofu on it.

"Where's the best pizza in town?" he asked, backing down Jimi's driveway. The car smelled brand-new. I don't understand why rental cars are new. They just get torn up. Why don't they rent out used cars?

Anyway, I gave Uncle Bob directions, and he drove. Then we sat while they made the pizza.

"Are we going to talk about Dad?" I asked. The pizza should have been ready by now.

"Whenever you want," Uncle Bob said. "I was able to meet his doctors this afternoon."

"Is he going to be OK?" I asked.

Uncle Bob took a deep breath and looked at his hands.

"Maybe we should wait until we get home," I said.

"Good idea," Uncle Bob said. "Besides, our pizza is ready. Let's just get it to go. We'll eat at your house."

I was on my second piece of pizza before I tried again.

"How's Mom?" I asked.

"Good," Uncle Bob said, wiping his chin. "Tired, I guess, but good."

"I didn't freak her out this morning?"

Uncle Bob smiled. "No, Isaac, you didn't. You did fine. It's tough to see what you saw. Especially when… well, you never really get used to it."

He wasn't smiling anymore.

"I didn't recognize him," I said. "I didn't recognize my own dad."

Uncle Bob had just taken another bite. He chewed for a while, then swallowed, then wiped his chin again.

"I had to sit for a while," he said, "before I could find my brother in there."

"What happened?" I asked. "He just had a little bump on his head—"

"Your father is pretty sick."

"And the eye thing?" I asked.

Uncle Bob finished his piece and held the box out to me. There was almost half a pizza left, but I didn't want any more. "It will be good to have leftovers," Uncle Bob had said when we ordered the extra large, extra thick.

He closed the lid on the box and walked into the kitchen. I could hear him put the box in the refrigerator, then wash his hands at the sink. When he came back, he was wiping his wet hands on his face. Dad always did the same thing. He said it was refreshing. I like to use a towel.

Uncle Bob sat down again, way in the back of his chair. It was obvious he planned to be there for a while.

"Let's start," he said, "with what you don't know."

I finished my pizza and wiped my hands with a paper towel. Then I wiped my mouth with another paper towel. I wadded up the towels and left them on the table. Then I sat back in my chair, too.

"When your dad fell off the roof," he said, pointing at the ceiling, "he landed pretty hard—"

"On the grass," I said. "Grass is soft."

"Maybe," said Uncle Bob, "but it's the end of summer, and I'll bet my brother hasn't watered for over a month, and the ground is probably pretty dry."

He had a point.

"But it doesn't matter much," he said. "A roof fall is a big fall."

I nodded.

"When he landed, he broke two ribs and ruptured some internal organs."

"Like his stomach?" I asked.

Uncle Bob smiled a little.

"His spleen and one kidney."

"He felt fine, though," I said, "just a little sore."

"It's normal for these things to hurt later," he said. "The doctors removed his spleen, repaired his kidney, and fixed the partial pneumothorax."

"What's a newmo-thing?" I asked.

Uncle Bob smiled. "Sorry. Collapsed lung. Air leaked from his lung into his chest cavity, and his lung collapsed a little. It's all fixed now, and his ribs will take some time to heal but those will be fine, too."

"Sounds great," I said. "So when does he come home?"

Uncle Bob smiled, then frowned. He made fists on top of his thighs.

"We're not done," he said.

"The bump," I said.

"And his eye," Uncle Bob said. "That's the big one."

"I've bumped my head a lot of times," I said, "and I'm perfectly normal, uhh, normal." I made a little head motion.

Uncle Bob didn't smile.

"When your dad landed, his head hit hard, maybe a rock in the lawn or something."

I thought for a minute.

"The patio," I said. "His head was right next to the patio."

"Maybe. Anyway, the sudden stop hurt him inside his skull more than outside his skull."

"So it's not the bump?" I asked.

"No. Somewhere inside his head, a blood vessel burst —tore open from the sudden stop."

We hear about this stuff when we get the bike helmet lecture every year in school.

"His brain sloshed around inside his head," I said.

"Right," said Uncle Bob. He looked a little surprised. "His skull stopped suddenly, but his brain kept moving. Some of the blood vessels and membranes connected between his brain and his body couldn't stretch enough and they tore. There may also be parts of his brain that tore, or sheared, apart from each other."

"So that messed up his eye controllers?"

Uncle Bob took a deep breath and sat for a second. Then he leaned forward again.

"Remember, two years ago, when you sprained your ankle really badly?"

"Yeah," I said, "that hurt. It hurt for almost two months."

"Right," Uncle Bob said. "Exactly. Remember how much it swelled up?"

I remember that really well. My ankle was almost as big at my foot. I nodded.

"OK, good, I'm glad you remember that," Uncle Bob said. "When your body gets injured, the injured area is flooded with fluid to wash away the injured material and provide a good growing environment for the repair tissue. Those fluids cause the swelling."

I nodded again. It was kind of a fake nod. I'd have to think about this later.

"But when your body gets hurt badly enough, the swelling creates problems by itself. In your dad's case, the brain injury caused his brain to swell. Plus, the torn artery was leaking blood into his head. But because the skull is rigid, all that extra fluid just squeezed his brain. The pressure can do lots of damage. It's what made his pupil dilate. It may affect his thinking, or his speech, or his motor skills, or cause other problems."

"So will they put ice on his head?" I didn't see any ice when I was there. We put ice on my sprained ankle for over a week straight.

"They actually removed a part of your dad's skull, in the back, to make room for his brain to expand, and they repaired the torn artery and drained off as much of the leaked blood as they could."

"So the pressure's gone?" I asked. That seemed pretty drastic.

"The pressure is reduced," he said. "They're also giving him drugs that should further decrease the swelling. They may even have made his brain colder to reduce the swelling, using fluids instead of ice. We can ask about that later, if you want."

Wow. They cut off the back of my dad's head. That explains the bad haircut and the mess.

"What about the tubes in his face?" I asked.

"The tube in his mouth is to keep his airway open and help him breathe," Uncle Bob said, "and his nasal tube goes all the way to his stomach. They use it to feed him."

Wow again.

"But he'll be OK?" I asked. "They'll put his skull back together and he'll be OK?"

Uncle Bob made the fists again.

"Isaac," he said, leaning forward, "this is really, really important. Your dad, my brother, has very good doctors who are doing all they can for him, but we won't know if he's OK until he wakes up, which will be at least a week or two. We may not know if he's OK for a few more months."

"But he could be fine," I said.

"Your dad is very sick," Uncle Bob said. "We just don't know, and we won't for some time."

"Is he going to die?" I asked.

"He did die," Uncle Bob said. "The doctors brought him back. But we just don't know how much damage was done to his brain from the fall and from the pressure on his brain after the fall."

"He died?"

Uncle Bob just nodded his head.

"But maybe he's fine, now," I said.

"Maybe," Uncle Bob said. "We don't know."

"Maybe," I said. My dad's tough. That was good enough for me.

Uncle Bob went to bed right after that, in the guest room. I made sure he had a clean pillowcase and stuff, then I went to bed, too.

I called Mom right before I went to bed, though. She was glad Uncle Bob and I had a talk. I was, too.

Dad would be fine.

Chapter 7:
Bedside Manner.

Uncle Bob stopped at the hospital on his way to the airport.

"I'll be back at the end of the week," he told Mom.

"Thanks for talking to Isaac," she said, "and thanks for being here."

"Not a problem," he told her.

Then he turned to me.

"Remember," he told me, with really serious eyes, "we won't know if your dad's OK for a while."

"But maybe he's fine," I said. "That's what you said last night."

Mom looked at me, then looked at Uncle Bob.

"Maybe," he said, "but not probably. We just don't know."

I smiled. I wasn't worried.

"See you in a week," I said. "Maybe we'll probably know by then."

Uncle Bob looked at me, then looked at Mom.

She shrugged.

"See you in a week," he said.

Then he gave me a quick hug, which was plenty, and he gave Mom a big hug.

Then he left, and we were alone in the hallway outside Dad's room.

"Are you ready to go back in?" she asked me. "You don't have to."

I just smiled. "All set," I said. "Uncle Bob explained everything. I just need to get used to it, that's all."

"Yes," Mom said, taking my arm, "we just need to get used to it."

Now that I knew what all the tubes were for, Dad didn't freak me out as much, although his face was still all swollen up and he didn't look very much like himself. The bruise on the left side of his face was darker, too. Almost solid purple.

I sat in the big blocky chair by the window and just watched. Mom sat in a smaller chair pulled right up against the bed. She held Dad's hand, and sometimes she used a tissue to wipe his face a little.

"His eyes water," she told me. "I don't want his crinkles to get chapped."

"No," I said. "Chapped crinkles would be bad."

Mom was squeezing my knee. I guess I'd fallen asleep.

"Isaac, honey," she said, "let's go. I need to go home and take a shower and get some clean clothes."

I blinked a few times and shook my head. Dad's room was kept pretty dark. It took me a while to get reoriented.

"I'll stay," I said.

Mom looked at me and kneeled down in front of the big chair.

"I think that's a bad idea," she said. "You should come with me. We'll be back right after lunch."

"I'll stay," I said. "Bring me a sandwich."

I didn't know why I was being so obnoxious. I could see that it hurt Mom.

"Please," I said.

Mom stood up and patted my hand.

"Come here," she said.

She led me over to Dad's bed and showed me a push button on the end of a long cord. It was pinned to the sheets right next to Dad's head.

"Use this if you need anything, or if anything weird happens or anything you don't understand happens," she said. "The nurses will come right away."

"Got it," I said. A nurse summoner.

"Now come to the door and give me a hug, then wipe your hands with the sterilizer."

Mom was gone, just like that.

I wiped my hands with way too much sanitizer, but by the time I reached for a paper towel, it had all dried away. Pretty cool stuff.

I went back and sat in the big chair by the window, but that didn't seem right, so I decided to sit by Dad's bed.

First I resanitized my hands again. I used the right amount of sanitizer this time.

I just sat and watched Dad for a while. The *wishhh-click* noise I'd heard at first was the machine that breathed for him. The air bubbled through a little bubbler half-full of water. I'd need to keep an eye on that, so no water got into Dad's lungs. Coughing would probably screw up all the machines. It looked OK for now.

The pulse machine was cool to watch, but it got boring pretty quickly. I guess Dad's pulse was OK.

He had a clip on the end of his middle finger on his right hand. The clip had a light in it and a wire coming out of it. I tried to follow the wire, but it got all mixed in with all the other stuff.

The clear water bags all drained into clear tubes. Each tube had a little pinch clamp right below the bag and then a drip-showing cup where you could see how fast it was flowing. Only one of them was dripping at all. The other two were clamped off completely. Spares, probably. Do we let one completely run out before starting the next? Can the water stop for a second or two before you start the next one? The nurses probably would know what to do.

I saw a little drop come out of the corner of Dad's left eye. A tear, I guess. I grabbed a tissue and dabbed it off his face. We didn't want his crinkles to chap.

I decided to hold Dad's hand, but I was still holding the tissue. I checked his eyes for dribbles, then walked over to the sink to throw the tissue away. Then I sanitized my hands again. Probably a tissue was pretty dirty.

Dad's hand was warm, which surprised me. I hadn't held his hand since I was a little kid. Our hands were almost the same size now, except my fingers were skinnier than his. I was putting my hand right over the top of his, to compare, when two ladies walked in.

"You the son?" asked the first one.

"Yes, ma'am," I said, "this is my dad."

Both ladies were rubbing sanitizer on their hands. It looked like they were using the right amount.

"Well," the first lady said, "we need to wash your dad. You should probably wait outside."

I backed away toward the window.

"No," I said. "I'll be fine, over here. I'll stay out of your way."

The first lady just looked at me, then looked at the second lady.

The second lady shrugged.

"All right," the first lady said, "but you really should wait outside."

"I'll be fine," I said. "Over here. I'll stay out of your way."

I'd never seen Dad naked before. One time, he got all wet when a sprinkler attacked him in the backyard and he left all his clothes on the back porch, but I only saw his butt. Seeing him all naked was very weird. He was fatter than I thought. Especially his belly. Plus, it was like he didn't have any muscles at all. The ladies washed his front, then rolled him one way and washed one side of his back, then the other way to wash the other side. Then they rolled him back and forth to change the sheet under him. I saw the stitches on the back of his head.

"All done, dear," the first lady said.

Also, that bag of orange-red liquid hanging under the bed was his pee. There was a hose that…it ran right to the bag.

The ladies reorganized all the wires and switches and put the hoses back where they were supposed to be, and they were gone in just a few moments.

I rubbed sanitizer on my hands again and pulled the chair back next to the bed. I guess I should have moved the chair first; chairs are probably pretty dirty. But I didn't.

I held Dad's hand some more and watched his eyes for more drips. I didn't see any.

I was thinking about moving to the other side of the bed when another lady came in. I started to get up.

"You're fine, sweetie," she said. "You can stay there." She was already wiping her hands together. Sanitizer quantity looked OK.

I didn't want to argue with her, so I sat back down. She checked the machines, one by one, and the drippers on the water bags. She tapped the dripping one with her fingernail and nodded a little. I started to ask her what they were for, but then she started to check the pulse machine and I didn't want to distract her. She put some goo on Dad's eyes, smiled at me, and left.

I sat for a while and held Dad's hand. If I squeezed, or didn't squeeze, or rubbed, or didn't rub, there was no change.

I put his hand down and tucked it under the blankets, and then I moved the chair to the other side of the bed. Then, because I carried the chair, I sanitized my hands again and went back and sat and held his other hand.

This side was harder, because of the clip on his finger. I didn't want to bump it off or make it slide. I just held his hand and didn't move and listened to the breathing machine.

Chapter 8:
Family.

Mom woke me up. My head was on the bed, and there was a big wet spot from my drool. That wasn't sanitary at all probably. Drool is full of germs.

Mom looked a lot better, though. Her hair was clean and all tied back, like in a ponytail except I don't know what to call it when it's on an old lady. She was even dressed in decent clothes.

"How's Dad doing," she said. "Everything good?"

I told her about the washing ladies and the machine-checking lady. I didn't tell her about the pee tube. She probably already knew. She probably didn't want to talk about it, either.

"Great job, Isaac," she said. "I'm very proud of you."

"All I did was sit," I said, "and use hand sanitizer. I wonder if we need to get some more?"

Mom laughed. "I'm sure we're fine. They'll bring more if we run out. Now why don't you take a walk, maybe eat the sandwich I left for you in the car, and I'll sit with Dad for a while. We're having dinner at the Petersons' tonight, too, so maybe you should go home and clean up."

"Clean up to eat at Jimi's house?" I said. "Not required. I'll go get my sammich and walk around a little. When do you want me back?"

Mom just smiled at me. Really a big smile.

"What?" I said.

"Thanks, Isaac," she said. "Thanks for being so strong."

That made me feel pretty good.

"You sure we can leave Dad here alone, tonight?" I said.

Mom looked down and touched the back of Dad's hand with her fingertips. "Yes," she said. "It is difficult to know what is the right thing to do. Sometimes it feels like we can only choose between bad and worse. We can go to Petersons' for dinner, though. Dad will be fine here."

Jimi & Isaac 5a:

Dinner at Jimi's house was great. Jimi's mom had just saved the whole lasagna from the other night and reheated it. It was a little bit dry around the edges, but everyone knows that lasagna leftovers are better than lasagna firsts, so a whole pan of leftover lasagna was the best.

Mom went back to the hospital after dinner, but Jimi's dad wanted to play his guitar with a drummer, so I stayed. It was great, too. I can't believe how good Jimi was getting on the saxophone. Maybe it's because he and his dad are related, but they sure sounded fantastic together.

"Your dad makes you sound good," I said to Jimi later, while we were getting ready for bed. Mom wanted me to sleep over instead of walking home late.

"Yeah," Jimi said, "he does. My constant practicing and intricate skills have nothing to do with it. It's weird, though, that he couldn't make your drum parts sound better. Usually he can fix anything."

That made me smile. Usually Jimi doesn't push back at all. Good for him.

"It's a shame really," I said. "At least I was loud, though. I'll always have volume to fall back on."

"Forward, too," Jimi said. "Whichever way you fall, you'll fall loudly."

That made me laugh. Jimi was getting snappy.

I finished spreading my sleeping bag on the floor and sat at Jimi's desk. It was quiet for a while.

"I'm sorry about your dad," Jimi said finally.

"I'm sorry, too," I said. "I can't wait until he gets better."

"He's going to get better?" Jimi said. "That's great!"

I just looked at him.

"Of course he's going to get better," I said.

I thought for a minute.

"Why?" I asked. "What did you hear?"

Jimi turned away from me, grabbed a shirt off the floor, and hung it up. "Nothing, I guess," he said to the closet.

Jimi has never hung up a shirt in the entire history of the earth. I just looked at him and waited. Eventually he turned around and faced me. He looked surprised that I was still looking at him.

"What did you hear?" I said.

"Mom…" he mumbled.

I just waited.

"My mom said that your mom said that your dad was pretty messed up, that he may never talk or walk again."

I smiled.

"Everyone says 'may never,' not 'won't' or 'can't,'" I said. "The doctors say maybe he'll be OK, or maybe he'll die again, or—"

"Die again?" Jimi asked. He forgot to close his mouth after that.

"Yeah," I said. "He died in surgery right after they got to the hospital, but they restarted him. He's fine.

They just can't say he's fine until after we can all see for ourselves he's fine. The doctors have to look good when it's over, so they cover all the bases."

Jimi just shrugged.

"Good night, Isaac," he said.

"Good night, Jimi the old woman," I said. "Don't worry. Dad's going to be fine."

"I hope so," he said.

"I know so," I said.

Chapter 9:
Please, God.

After breakfast, I walked home and changed clothes, then I walked to the hospital. It was nice to do a little walking. I'd been sitting too much lately.

"I hope you said thank you to Mrs. Peterson before you left," Mom said when I finally got to the hospital. She was waiting for me in the coffee shop. She wasn't drinking coffee, though. Tea, I think.

"Absolutely," I told her, "except for the 'Mrs.' part." She just looked at me.

"Jimi's mom was gone already when we got up," I said. "But I said thank you to Jimi's dad. I even made him breakfast."

Mom smiled. "Your famous oatmeal?"

"Isaac Instant," I said. "With raisins and brown sugar. He said I'm the only cook that gives him sugar. He thinks I should stay over more often."

Mom smiled again but more like a real smile this time. Which reminded me...

"I saw Mrs. Morgan on the way to the hospital, too," I said.

This time Mom smiled for real.

"How is she doing?" Mom said. "And how is Spoodle the wonder dog of science?"

"Spoodle is good," I said, "but he's getting old. He can't get onto the front porch in one jump. He needs to use the steps."

It was nice to see Mom smile.

"And he's not 'the wonder dog of science' anymore. Just 'Solar Spoodle.' It's shorter and fits better on the T-shirts we're having printed. They'll be for sale right next to the Spoodle private label dog toys and Spoodle Poop Shovels."

Finally, Mom laughed. She knew that even though Spoodle was a key contributor to development of the world's greatest solar panels, there would never be any logo wear. We could never discuss Spoodle's contribution in public.

"Mrs. Morgan knew all about Dad," I said.

Mom's smile got smaller again.

"She said she'd pray for him."

Mom looked at her hands and twisted her wedding ring. Her hands were red and dry. Probably too much sanitizer.

"That would be good," Mom said.

I didn't expect that.

"I thought you and Dad didn't believe in God," I said.

Mom spun her ring a couple more times. Finally she looked up at me.

"Dad and I don't talk about it much," she said, "but we both believe in God. We just don't know who he is —what he is—what it is."

Wow.

"Why don't we go to church, then?" I asked.

Mom straightened her ring.

"Dad and I do agree on that," she said. "We don't like church."

"Mrs. Morgan goes to church," I said, "all the time."

"Good," Mom said. "Church seems to be good for some people. Just not for Dad and me."

Mom sipped her tea.

"Jimi thought that Dad would never get better."

Mom just looked into her mug.

"He said that's what you told his mom."

She didn't even move, except her hands tightened up a little.

Finally she looked up.

"I thought you and Uncle Bob talked about this," she said.

"Yeah," I said, "we did. He said we need to wait until Dad wakes up. Then we'll know he's OK."

Mom looked into her mug again. I was pretty sure it was empty.

"We know," Mom said, "that your dad's brain is injured. Possibly just a little. Probably seriously. Maybe very seriously."

I probably should have said something, but I didn't. I was stuck.

"We won't know how extensive the damage is until he wakes up."

She stopped again. Her hands were super tight on the mug.

"I'll talk to Uncle Bob again when he gets here," I said.

Mom looked at me. Her eyes were really red.

"You need to understand this, Isaac. I wish I could tell you that everything is fine, but it's not. It's horrible. You need to understand."

She tried to let go of her tea. Her fingers got tight and loose and tight and loose. All jerky.

"I'll just talk to Uncle Bob," I said.

"Isaac," she said, "listen to me. We don't know how much the fall damaged your father's brain. It's possible that he'll be home in a couple of months, and that he'll need help relearning how to use some muscles and speak clearly. It's more likely that he'll be unable to do some things for himself, like washing and eating and…"

"…and going to the bathroom?" I asked. I was thinking about the pee tube.

"That," Mom said. Then she got quiet again.

"Then we'll help him," I said.

"Isaac," she said very quietly, "listen to me. It may be much worse…"

She had more to say, I could tell. But she stopped.

Worse than a pee tube?

"I gotta go," I said. "I'll be at home."

Mom looked into the bottom of her mug.

"Isaac," she said very, very quietly, "I love you. Your dad loves you. We know you love us. We'll get through this."

I stood up.

"I gotta go," I said.

Chapter 10:
Lies.

"You lied to me!" I yelled.

Uncle Bob just sat there. Like a lump. Like a lying lump.

I wanted to talk to him, to find out what was true, but I couldn't. His suitcase was sitting on the floor next to him. He'd only been in the house for ten seconds, and I was screaming.

"You said my dad was fine!" I knew that wasn't really right but still. "You said he'd be fine!"

"That's not what I…" The lying lump waved his hands.

"My father," I yelled, "is in the hospital, and you're lying to me!"

"Slow down a second, Isaac," the lump said. "Please, just sit down and we'll talk."

The lump pulled out the chair next to him at the breakfast table.

I grabbed at the chair and tore it out of his hand. Then the chair kept going. By the time it stopped, it was tipped over and stuck into the wall, there was a big hole in the drywall, and the chair and the floor were covered in white dust.

I just looked at him. I thought it was as bad as it could get, and now it was worse.

Then I started shaking. Shaking and crying. Like a baby. My whole face was wet, and I could barely stand up.

Uncle Bob looked terrible. His face was broken. He was trying to smile, but it wasn't working. It looked like his face didn't know what to do.

I screamed and left the room. I screamed like an idiot, and I left. I made it worse. Everything kept getting worse

"I'm sorry, Mom," I said later. I'd been lying in my bed for most of the morning. At first, I just cried, but I guess I fell asleep.

She just sat there on the edge of my bed and didn't move, except she squeezed my shoulder a little.

"It's OK that you're angry," she said very quietly.

"I'm sorry I yelled at Uncle Bob."

"Me, too," she said. "He's hurting just as much as we are, you know."

I had to think about that for a while.

"I should go apologize to him," I said.

"He's not here," Mom said. "He's at the hospital with his brother."

I thought for a minute.

"With Dad."

Mom took a deep breath and exhaled really slowly.

"With your father," she said.

I sat up and faced her.

"Mom," I said, as quietly as I could, "we need to move Dad to a good hospital, where they know what they're doing. I'll start looking around on the Internet right away." I didn't do a very good job being quiet, but at least I wasn't yelling. I wanted to yell.

"He's at a good hospital," she said. "A very good hospital."

"They don't know what they're doing," I said, trying very, very hard to not yell. "They don't even know what's wrong with Dad, or else they're hiding what's really going on."

Mom started to reach her hand toward my shoulder again, but then she stopped and put both her hands in her lap. Her hands were all red and chapped. There were cracks on the back of her knuckles.

"Isaac," she said quietly. "Isaac, look at me."

I looked up from her hands. Her eyes were as red as her knuckles.

"Isaac," she said, "the doctors working on your father are among the best in the world. We know some of them from the university. I trust each and every one of them."

"Then why don't they help Dad?" I said. "Why won't they make him better?"

"Not everything can be fixed," she said finally.

We sat for a long time. Mom's nose was running. She had to get a tissue off my desk.

"I'm going back to the hospital," she said. "Can you get your own dinner?"

I nodded. She left.

I was in my room when I heard Uncle Bob come into the house and go to the guest room. I didn't get up and say good night. He didn't knock on my door, either.

Chapter 11:
No Babies.

Uncle Bob was at the breakfast table the next morning, reading a book. I fixed a bowl of cereal and sat across from him.

"Sorry about the yelling," I said.

Uncle Bob looked up at me and sat back in his chair.

"Me, too," he said, "and I'm sorry about the misunderstanding, too."

I ate my cereal for a while. It seemed like the crunchiness was more crunchy that usual. I tried to eat quieter.

"Is Mom at the hospital?" I asked.

Uncle Bob nodded. "Yeah," he said, "she is. We probably won't see her today or tonight, either. Maybe you and me can get some projects done today."

I just looked at him. I didn't want to do any projects.

He made a little jerk motion with his head and rolled his eyes. I followed the movement.

"I don't know how to fix walls," I said.

"I do," he said, "and you'll learn. Plus there's a bunch of loose stuff still on the roof. We need to get everything secured up there and get the panels hooked up."

"Not going to happen," I said. "Dad and I are installing the solar panels. It's a father-son thing. I'll wait until he's ready."

"You'll wait awhile," Uncle Bob said. "Your dad won't be ready for ladders for a long, long, time."

"Maybe never," I said.

Uncle Bob nodded slowly.

"Then they'll never get hooked up," I said. "That's fine with me."

"Fine with me as well," Uncle Bob said finally, "but we need to make sure everything is fastened securely and all the loose tools are picked up."

I thought about it for a moment.

"You're right," I said. "We need to make it safe."

Uncle Bob sipped his coffee.

"Finish your cereal," he said, "we need to go to the store. You need some special wall-fixing stuff."

"*We* need," I said.

Uncle Bob just smiled and went back to his reading.

Patching the hole in the wall was not that big of a deal, really. Uncle Bob seemed to know what he was doing, but he made me do most of the work. Probably trying to protect his hands so he could still be a doctor.

Cleaning off the roof was easy, too. We just had to recheck that Dad and I got all the screws in all the panels and carry the tools down. Everything was cool.

"I think I'll walk over to the hospital," I said. "I'll paint the wall patch later, like you told me."

Uncle Bob checked his watch. "Why don't you hang out here for another hour or so?" he said. "Your mom is supposed to call me then, and we'll see what she wants to do for the rest of the day."

"I'll just see her at the hospital," I said. "No big deal."

Uncle Bob made a serious face.

"Isaac," he said, "your mom wants to be alone with your father today. She…"

"Is it because of our yelling yesterday?" I asked. "I'll tell her I'm sorry. She knows I'm sorry."

Uncle Bob's face got seriouser.

"No, Isaac, that's not the problem," he said. "Your dad's doctors are trying something today. They're reducing the sedation, the drugs that are keeping your dad asleep, to see what happens."

"I should be there," I said. "I need to be there when he wakes up!"

Uncle Bob held up both his hands, with his palms toward me.

"Slow down, Isaac," he said. "First of all, it's your mom's decision. All of this, everything we do, is about doing what your mom wants."

He looked at me. I could tell he knew I wanted to smash his face.

"Right?" he said. "It's about supporting your mom."

Finally I took a breath. I suddenly felt really tired.

"Right," I said.

"Secondly," Uncle Bob said, "your dad probably won't wake up all the way, even if everything is great. They'll keep him pretty heavily sedated so he doesn't move around and tear out all the needles and tubes they have stuck in him, and so the swelling in his brain continues to decrease. They may not see any outward physical signs of consciousness. It may be pretty subtle."

"It's not right," I said. "I should be there. He's my dad."

Uncle Bob dropped his hands.

"Yeah," he said. "We should be there. But we'll wait here, for your mom to call."

He just stood there, looking at me.

"OK," I said. We'll wait.

Chapter 12:
Set Back.

Mom finally called. She didn't talk to me; she only talked to Uncle Bob.

The seizure had been huge inside his brain, like a lightning and thunder storm, Uncle Bob said, but Dad's muscles were still paralyzed because of all the medicines, so he didn't move.

It wasn't good.

"It wasn't bad, either," Uncle Bob said, "he's just not ready to be conscious. They'll adjust his meds and try again in a few days."

"I thought you weren't going to lie to me anymore," I said. I was pretty sure I was going to have to fight my uncle. He just wasn't getting it. I needed to know what was going on.

"I'm not lying to you, Isaac," he said. "Not at all. I'm telling you every bit of the truth."

"Pretending something is OK when it's really bad is lying," I said.

"Sometimes," he said. "Sometimes you need to consider other issues. But I'm not doing that here, Isaac. It's certainly not good news that your dad had a seizure, but it's not unexpected, either."

"He's going to be a vegetable," I said. "He's going to lie there completely helpless, and we're going to wipe his tears and his drool and his…"

I started crying again, but it didn't last long.

Uncle Bob was shaking me by the shoulders. Pretty hard.

"Isaac! Isaac!"

I stopped blubbering and looked up at my uncle. He was right in my face.

"Listen to me, Isaac! I love you and I love your mom, and I want to help you," he said, "but don't you ever, ever call my brother a vegetable."

"I just…"

"He's a man," Uncle Bob said. "A very, very sick man. He needs you, and me, and all of us around him to support him."

"I didn't mean…"

"You wanted me to tell you the truth," Uncle Bob said. He wasn't yelling, but it felt like he was yelling. "Well, I told you the truth. The ugly, uncomfortable, and frustrating truth. So we're going to talk to each other and tell each other the truth, and we're going to get through this!"

I nodded.

"But," he said, his voice finally getting quiet, "we are going to remember that your father is a man. He is not a thing."

His eyes were hard. I'd never seen Uncle Bob with hard eyes before.

I sniffed and looked back at him.

"I love my dad," I said.

"I love your dad, too," he said.

Chapter 13:
Regroup.

Mom didn't want us at the hospital.

I didn't want to talk to Uncle Bob.

So I went to Jimi's house.

"You here for dinner?" Jimi asked.

"If it's OK," I said.

"Of course," Jimi said. "I'll tell Dad."

He was back in just a few seconds.

"Just us guys," he said. "Mom and Janis are at the hospital, with your mom."

"Mom didn't want visitors," I said.

Jimi looked at me for a second, then shrugged.

"Dunno," he said, "but they're gone anyway."

Jimi's dad was just starting a guitar lesson in the basement. Beginning guitar, it sounded like. Maybe the first day.

"Fifth month," Jimi said.

"Wow," I said. "Still playing open chords?"

Jimi just laughed a little.

"Dad plays open chords all the time," Jimi said. "He says his fingers are getting too stiff to play barre."

That was funny. "The day your dad can't play whatever he wants to play…"

Jimi stopped laughing. "No, really," he said, "he's getting arthritis in his fingers."

That was not good news.

"Our dads are getting old," I said.

"Yeah," Jimi said, "time for the new blood to take over."

"Fresh meat," I said. "The universe craves fresh meat."

Jimi laughed.

"Hey!" he yelled, jumping up and running out of the living room. "Check this out!"

I got out of my chair and started to follow him, but he was already coming back. I got out of his way.

He waved a little card in my face.

"Learner's permit, baby!" he yelled. He had a huge smile on his face.

"Cool," I said. "You're in the new driver's ed class?"

"Yep," he said. "We start driving right after school starts."

I just shook my head. "This town isn't ready," I said.

"It's already started," Jimi said. "Dad took me driving last night."

I just looked at him for a while.

"You start soon, right?" he said.

I nodded. "Next class," I said. "That was the plan, at least."

"No sweat," Jimi said. "My dad will drive you if your dad's not ready yet."

"It's not that important," I said. "But Mom might let me drive her around. She hates driving."

"My mom hates driving, too." Jimi laughed. "But she hates letting me drive more. I don't think she'll be riding with me for a long, long time. Maybe never."

We just sat there for a while. I could hear the guitars from the basement. Jimi's dad played easy and smooth, but the student was horrible. "G-A-D? Really?"

Jimi laughed again. "He's not Dad's worst student," Jimi said. "At least it sounds like music. Sometimes his students can't even hear what they're playing. Dad gets pretty frustrated then."

"Does he tell them to quit?" I asked. He should tell them to quit.

"No," Jimi said, "of course not. Dad thinks everyone should play music, all the time. Besides, Dad can't just stop giving lessons. We need the money..."

I just looked at Jimi. I wasn't sure if he was joking. Jimi just looked back.

We just sat there, looking at each other.

"The solar panels," I said.

"Yeah," Jimi said, "are they making you money yet?"

"Not really," I said, "but Mom gets paid a lot to teach, and she has tenure."

"What does that mean?" Jimi asked.

"It means they can't fire her," I said.

It got quiet again.

"Even if she's home taking care of your dad?" Jimi asked.

I didn't know the answer to that. I didn't want to talk about it, either. If the solar panels didn't start making money soon, there wasn't much I could do about it.

Except not go to college. That would save some money.

"If I have to," I said, "I won't go to college."

Jimi just smiled. He even snickered a little. "I'm pretty sure you're going to college," Jimi said.

"Yeah."

The guitars were still playing. Jimi's dad was just chunking along with the 12-bar blues, and the other guy was trying to play along. Horrible.

Finally, Jimi's dad played a little turnaround and closed it off. The quiet felt good.

"Soccer starts Monday," Jimi said finally. "*High school* soccer."

"Yeah," I said, "big deal."

"Big, big deal," Jimi said. "Ninety-minute games, huge fields, decent refs, wicked fouls, fistfights, everything you're good at."

I just smiled.

"Probably not," I said.

"Probably not what?" Jimi asked, like his head was filled with concrete.

"Dad's sick," I said. "No soccer this year."

"Our goalie's a senior," Jimi said, "and you're already better than him. You're bigger than he is, too. You have to play."

I just looked at Jimi.

"It doesn't matter," I said.

Jimi's mouth was open.

"Of course it matters," he said. "Don't be stupid!"

"It's just soccer," I said.

"Says nobody, ever."

"Shut up, Jimi," I said. "Shut up now!"

"Don't be stupid, stupid," Jimi said again. "Soccer starts Monday. *High school* soccer starts Monday."

I didn't want to hurt him, so I left.

"Isaac," Jimi yelled from his front door, "come back here!"

It was like the most ridiculous drama ever.

"Isaac!"

I walked home. There wasn't anyplace else to go.

Chapter 14:
Real.

"Of course you're going," Mom said.

Jimi probably told his mom, and his mom probably told my mom.

"No way, Mom," I said. "Uncle Bob told me about the seizure yesterday. Dad needs me to be with him. Maybe I can help."

Mom smiled, then frowned. I think frowning feels better for her. Maybe it hurts to smile.

"You can help, dear," she said. "So sit with your dad until lunchtime, then walk home and get your gear. Uncle Bob will drop you off at soccer practice before he comes here to the hospital. Then he has to fly home again tonight."

"He's not spending much time with his brother," I said. "With Dad, I mean."

"No," Mom said, "he's not. I think he wants to stay out of our way. I think he feels uncomfortable."

Good, I thought. But that felt pretty mean.

"Were the seizures…?" I asked.

Mom squeezed her hands in her lap.

"I didn't really see anything," she said. "Your father was still sedated."

"He couldn't move," I said.

"Right," she said, "but the doctors could tell, I guess. They said we'll just need to wait."

"Some more," I said.

"Some more," she said. "Probably a lot more."

The washing ladies came in again, right after Mom left. I was trying to hold Dad's hand, but I couldn't figure it out. It felt like I wasn't doing it right.

I recognized one of the ladies. Her helper was different, though, I think.

"You still gonna stay?" the lady asked.

I nodded. "Yeah," I said, "I'll be fine."

I went and stood by the window, looking out, but then I decided that I should watch. If Dad had to go through it, I could at least be there. It wasn't a big deal,

and Uncle Bob was right: Dad needed our support.
Even if that meant watching.

Besides, I figured, I would probably have to help
wash him after we brought in home, until his brain got
all better.

"I can help," I said. "I should learn how to help."

The washing lady looked at me. I could only see her
eyes, because she had a mask over her mouth.

"They'll teach you," she said. "When he's ready to go
home, they'll teach you."

I tried to watch closely, though, and see what they
did. They moved pretty fast. Changing the sheet was the
most amazing part. It takes me a whole morning to put
new sheets on my bed. Usually Mom does it for me,
because I'm so slow. She thinks I'm slow on purpose,
but I'm not. Maybe I am. Anyway, they changed the
sheets with Dad still in the bed. It didn't take them any
time at all.

There was a lot to learn.

After they left, I went back and sat with Dad. I didn't
hold his hand or touch him. I just sat by the bed.

It was pretty boring. The *wisssh-click* of the breathing
machine didn't help, either. It didn't get louder or
quieter or disappear or get more interesting. It just was.

They probably made it boring like that so sick people
would sleep better. If it was a snappier sound, with a
little syncopation or maybe more of a shuffle rhythm,

they'd probably need to give the sick people more drugs to keep them asleep. If they really fixed the machine, sick people would be snapping their fingers or dancing or something, and they'd never get any rest.

Finally the other lady came in to check the machines.

She tapped on the dripper and wiped inside the thing that was clipped on Dad's finger. Then she reached across to put some greasy stuff on Dad's eyes.

Then Dad farted. Really loud. It was embarrassing.

The lady just finished with the eye goo, wiped her fingers on some tissue, and then reached under Dad's pillow and pushed the nurse button.

It was really starting to smell. Dad really stunk the place up.

The lady smiled at me.

"You should probably wait for us outside," she said.

"No big deal," I said. "Dad farts. Farts smell. I get that."

"Oh, honey," she said. Another lady walked into the room and started putting on a gown and some gloves. "Your dad had a bowel movement. We need to clean him up."

Oh. I thought about it for a minute.

"No," I said, "I need to learn how to take care of him. I'll stay."

"You really should wait outside," she said.

Yeah, I thought, *but still...*

"I'll watch from over here," I said, sliding over to the chair by the window.

The other nurse came over to the bed, rolling a cart with her. The cart had cloth bins to put the dirty sheets in. The washing ladies had used it earlier. Bringing it right up to the bed was probably a good idea.

They pulled the top sheet off my dad, and he was lying there, completely naked, and there was a huge brown mess spreading out from under his butt and his legs. It looked like the medicine and the getting food pumped into his stomach gave him massive diarrhea. Massive. I could see the pee tube, too.

"I have soccer practice," I said. "I have to go."

"No problem, dear," the lady said. "We'll be fine."

I almost ran out of the hospital. I didn't help Dad.

Chapter 15:
Not Up. Not Down.

Mom was home when Jimi's sister dropped me off after practice.

"How did it go?" she asked.

"I panicked," I said. "I couldn't help."

She just looked at me.

"Dad crapped all over himself, and I ran away. I didn't help clean him up. I just ran."

She wrinkled her nose and scrunched her mouth, then smiled. "No," she said. "Not that. Soccer practice. How did soccer practice go?"

"Fine," I said. "I played well. I didn't fool around or anything."

Mom smiled.

"You're growing up," she said.

"I didn't have any fun, either," I said. "I don't think I'll play this year."

"Isaac," she said really quietly, "I don't think either one of us is going to enjoy our lives for a while. That doesn't mean we should stop living them, though."

"I don't mind," I said. "It's just soccer. I'll play next year."

"Do you think," Mom said, "that Dad would agree with that decision, or do you think that he would want you to keep doing the things that are important to you?"

"I think Dad…" I said. "As long as Dad needs to wear a diaper, I don't think he cares much what I do."

Mom made a face. Then she just…deflated.

"I need to take care of Dad," I said. "I don't need to play soccer."

Chapter 16:
Gardens.

"Good to see you, Mr. Farmer!"

Mrs. Morgan was weeding her flower garden. Mrs. Morgan is always weeding her flower garden. I don't think she likes flowers. I think she likes weeding.

I smiled and waved a little, then walked across her lawn to where she was working. Spoodle, her little gray dog, woke up on the front porch and ran inside the house.

"How's your father?" she asked. "I pray for his health."

"My dad can't chew food," I said. "And he craps himself."

"Isaac," Mrs. Morgan said, "don't be a jerk."

I get called a jerk a lot, I suppose, but I'd never heard it from Mrs. Morgan.

She wasn't done, though.

"People have problems," she said. "They wet themselves, they act badly, they have bad breath, they don't dress well, they don't know how to act in social situations…"

"My dad doesn't have little problems like that," I said. "My dad's brain is broken."

"I broke my leg when I was your age," she said. "The bone healed, and I walked again."

"It's not the same," I said. "They can't…"

Spoodle the wonder dog dropped a fabric duck at my feet. The stuffing was gone, and he had ripped the feet off long ago.

"…It's not the same."

Spoodle picked the duck up, shook it, and dropped it again.

I scooped it out of the grass with my left toe and flipped it away. Spoodle almost caught it in the air.

"How's soccer this year?" Mrs. Morgan said while Spoodle brought the duck back. "High school, right?"

I flipped the duck again, this time with my right toe.

"I'm supposed to be there now," I said, twisting a little so she could see my backpack. "I'm supposed to be the star goalie."

The duck was back. I stepped on the tail.

"You should get going, then," Mrs. Morgan said. "Spoodle will be here when you get back."

I shrugged. "Mom's making me go. I don't want to play this year."

Spoodle had the duck's head and was pulling. Pulling hard. I raised my foot off the duck. Spoodle barely moved. I guess it's easy to not fall backward if you have four legs.

"Because of your dad?"

I shrugged again.

"He wants you to play, I'm sure," she said.

"Dad won't know either way," I said. "He's all drugged up."

"How do you know that he doesn't know?"

"He doesn't move or react to anything. He just lies there in bed. A machine pumps air into his lungs—he doesn't even do his own breathing."

Spoodle took his duck onto the front porch. He didn't used to get bored that easily.

"That must be hard for you to see," she said quietly.

I went and sat next to Spoodle. Spoodle flipped the duck into my lap.

I took a deep breath, let it out as slowly as I could, and then breathed in again. I really didn't want to cry.

"It's worse for him," I said.

Mrs. Morgan walked over and sat next to me. She pulled off her gardening gloves, then put them and her little weeding rake on the step between her feet.

"What do you do when you visit your father?"

I looked over at her. Her eyes were red, and the eyelids were wrinkled and sore-looking.

"I sit and talk," I told her.

She just looked at me.

"I sit," I said. "There's no reason to talk."

Mrs. Morgan picked her gloves up and twisted them together, like she was wringing them out.

"I used to sit with Mr. Morgan," she said, "and hold his hand—"

Mrs. Morgan was looking at me. I tried to pay attention better.

"Mr. Morgan had a stroke," she said. "Many years ago. It took him from me, but I was glad to have a few days at the end where we could just sit together."

I nodded.

"I would hold his hand, and I would tell him about my day. I talked more to him in that hospital than I ever talked anywhere to anyone."

She looked at me. Finally I nodded again.

Mrs. Morgan smiled, then looked at her hands.

"I'm sorry," she said. "I guess I talked too much about talking."

"No," I said quickly, but then I just waited. It was pretty quiet.

"Did he hear you?" I asked.

She smiled at me.

"I think so," she said. "I hope so."

"You know," I said, "Dad used to be our soccer coach, back when we were kids. He liked—likes—to watch me play goalie. He'll want to hear about the high school team."

Mrs. Morgan smiled and got up, then turned and held out her hand.

"You better get going," she said.

I took her hand, and she leaned way back to drag me to my feet.

When I stood, Spoodle's duck fell out of my lap and onto the ground. I kneeled down and hooked it with a finger, then laid it across the snout of the great and powerful Spoodle. He stretched and snored, but he didn't wake up.

Mrs. Morgan was already back to her weeding.

"Make us all proud," she said. "Kick ass!"

"Yes, ma'am," I said, laughing. I didn't move, though.

Mrs. Morgan put the weeding rake down, rolled back on her heels, and looked back over her shoulder.

"Thanks for praying for Dad," I said.

She smiled and brushed her cheek with the back of her hand.

"I pray for you, too," she said. "Every day."

"I..." My mouth wasn't working.

"Thanks," I said.

Chapter 17:
Soccer Practice.

High school soccer was rough. No kid stuff. When we ran laps, we ran hard. When we worked a drill, we didn't fool around. At all. The coach stayed out of it, too. Mostly the practice was run by team captains— older kids that knew what was. The coach just called the drills and then walked around and made little comments. We hardly knew he was there.

One of the captains was Caleb, last year's goalie. I guess nobody told him that I would be starting this year.

"You suck," he said. I was stretched out on the ground, having just deflected a rocket our most powerful forward had just launched from the top of the penalty area. My hand hurt, too.

"Catch the shots," he said. "It's not enough to just punch them away. If you let the ball rebound, you give the other guys a goal."

I stood straight and walked right past him, looking down into his eyes. It was his turn in goal. We each took ten shots or so in goal, then traded out.

He stopped the shots, too. Five went wide or over the top, but he caught the five that were on goal. He pinched the last one against the ground, stopping it with one hand.

"Do you have sticky on your gloves?" I asked, moving back into the goal mouth.

He shook his head. "No," he said, "I don't use spray —it just collects dirt. These gloves are new. I'll get another pair once the season starts. They get slick pretty fast."

I looked down at my gloves. Dad bought them for me at the start of last season. He ordered them online. Somewhere-I-don't-know-where, online. The palm pads were made out of a bright orange soft plastic. They were really sticky, like Spider-Man sticky, last year. Now they were hard and smooth, like a car seat.

The first two shots went high, but I jumped at them anyway. I was able to get my fingers on the second one, tipping it higher over the goal, clear of the crossbar. It was good practice to go for everything, and it didn't hurt to show how much taller than Caleb I was.

"You just gave the other team a corner kick, genius," Caleb said. "Keep yourself under control."

The next shot was right at my head. Instead of punching it out, I tried to catch it. The ball blew through my hands.

"Thumbs together," Caleb yelled.

"I got it," I yelled back.

The next one went wide left, and I didn't move. No need to. After that, it was wide right. I just waved at it. Caleb didn't say a word.

"Ball!" someone yelled from outside the penalty area.

I waved, and he flipped the ball forward and into the air with his toe, then moved forward one step and drilled the ball before it landed.

It was a perfect volley kick, chest high with just a tiny bit of topspin. I started left just as the ball dipped and curled back to my right. It hit the ground at the same time I got my left hand down, but I got my feet up and blocked the ball. I scrambled after it and smothered it before it cleared the goalie box. It was pretty much a perfect play, but nobody said a word. I just stood up and rolled the ball back toward the players waiting at the top of the penalty area. When I looked back, Caleb had his head down, rooting around in his gear bag.

The next four shots were weak. I stopped them easily.

"Oohh, ahhh," Caleb said sarcastically when we switched places.

"You missed my best stop," I said. "Pro style."

"I'm sure you were great," Caleb said, moving into the goalmouth. "I left some gloves for you, Einstein…" He waved his hand at me.

I looked around.

"Where?" I said.

Caleb caught an easy shot between his hands, made an exaggerated windmill bowling motion, and rolled it back into the crowd of shooters.

"Just look," he said, "right by the back post."

I looked around.

"Nope," I said. "I don't see them."

Caleb rolled back off his toes and turned, then pointed at the back corner of the goal.

I followed his point, spotted the gloves, then turned and gave Caleb the thumbs-up.

He turned back toward the field just in time to see an incredibly powerful shot headed right at him. He was barely able to get his right hand up before the ball crushed his right hand into the right side of his head. There was a snapping noise, like a wooden pencil breaking, the ball bounced back into the field, and Caleb started screaming.

Chapter 18:
Back at the Hospital.

I stopped by the emergency room when I got to the hospital after dinner. The nurses at the desk pointed toward one of the rooms and let me go back by myself.

"Hey, Einstein!" Caleb said. He was holding an icepack over his right eye, with his right hand, but his right hand was all wrapped up in a tan elastic bandage.

I just looked at him. What a mess.

"Mom," Caleb said, "this is Einstein, the new varsity goalie."

"Hello," she said. She got out of her chair and walked toward me with her hand out.

"I didn't see you," I said, which was pretty stupid, "when I came in." Which was more stupid.

"Einstein?" She shook my hand.

Caleb laughed, then grunted, then moaned, then adjusted the icepack on his face.

"Isaac, ma'am," I said. "Isaac Farmer."

"Good to meet you, Isaac Farmer. I hope you're a good goalie."

Caleb laughed again, and grunted again, and moaned again.

"Are you OK?" I asked.

"Nope," his mom said, returning to her chair. "He's not OK."

"Except for the two broken fingers and the broken wrist and the black eye and the brain damage," Caleb said, "I'm just fine."

"So they splinted your fingers," I said, "and they'll cast them next week?"

"That's right," Caleb said. "How did you know?"

"The swelling has to go down," I said, "before they can put the cast on."

"Maybe you do know everything, Einstein," Caleb said.

I just smiled a little. "I wish I didn't know that," I said.

Caleb's mom spoke up. "Are you Professor Farmer's boy?"

"Yeah," I said. "Yes, I mean. He's my dad."

"I'm sorry, dear. Are you here to visit?"

"I'm on my way upstairs," I said. "But I wanted to see if Caleb was OK. The whole thing was kind of my fault."

Caleb snorted. "Anything to play varsity, right, Einstein?"

"It wasn't on purpose," I said. "I didn't mean to distract you."

Caleb snorted again. "Don't give yourself so much credit, Einstein. We could do the same thing every day for a year without anyone getting hurt. It's just the breaks."

"Ha-ha."

"Ha-ha is right. Tomorrow will be bad, though, I think—once the pain medicine wears off."

"They'll give you more," I said, "if you whine enough."

Caleb laughed, then moaned. Apparently laughing was bad for his face.

His mom giggled.

"Your dad's here?" Caleb asked.

"Yeah," I said, "he's upstairs in intensive care." He's…recovering. He fell off our roof two weeks ago."

"Wow," Caleb said. "That's rough. I hope he's feeling better."

"Me, too," I said.

Caleb's lowered his hand a little. His eye was one big purple mess.

"We don't know yet," I said. "He hit his head, and he's been unconscious since he fell. He's in a coma."

Caleb's eyes went a little empty, then narrowed again. "Hey, Isaac, I'm real sorry about that 'brain damage' crack. I didn't mean anything by it."

I looked at my feet and put my hands in my pockets. "You didn't know," I said. "I don't talk about it."

Caleb looked real sad.

"It's fine, really." I said. After that, it was quiet. "I need to get upstairs, sorry."

Caleb stuck out his left hand. "Thanks for coming by, Einstein. I'll see you at practice tomorrow."

"You're going to play?" I asked. There was no way he was going to play soccer tomorrow. Maybe he did have brain damage. Maybe it was the pain drugs.

"I'm going to coach," he said. "You've got a lot to learn."

I shook hands with Caleb left-handed.

"Can I wear your new gloves?" I asked.

Caleb smiled and frowned at the same time. I think his head was sore.

"See you tomorrow," I said.

By the time I turned around, Caleb's mom was between me and the door.

"It was good to meet you, Isaac," she said, shaking my right hand. "You're a fine young man. Your parents must be very proud of you."

I didn't cry.

"I hope so," I said.

Chapter 19:
More to Learn.

I hadn't met the guy working on Dad before. I just walked past him and sat in the chair by the window.

"You're Isaac?" he said. He had Dad's left leg in his hands, bending and unbending the knee. Dad's foot was totally floppy.

I nodded but then decided the guy wasn't watching when I nodded.

"I'm Isaac," I said.

"Do you have any questions about what I'm doing?" the guy asked. He stopped moving Dad's leg and reached down and adjusted the sheet so I couldn't see Dad's pee tube.

"No," I said, "not really. You're moving his legs so he doesn't get blood clots?"

The guy just looked at me. Finally I shrugged.

"That's right," he said. "We manipulate...move your dad's extremities twice a day to try and keep the blood flowing and the muscles active."

"Deep vein..." I couldn't remember the last word.

"Deep vein thrombosis," he said. "DVT. If the blood doesn't move enough, it can clot, which means it turns into a solid—"

"I know what a clot is," I said.

"Good. Well, the clots can form in his legs and arms, then break loose and flow to his heart—"

"Or his brain," I said.

The guy stopped talking and started working Dad's right leg.

"Sorry," I said, but the guy was done talking for a while.

"Will you put the bags on his legs, too?" I asked.

The guy flexed Dad's leg twice more, then laid it straight and spread the sheet and blanket. Then he moved up to Dad's right arm.

"We actually started using the pneumatic stockings on your dad five days ago, once it looked like he might be staying with us for a while. They're on him almost all the time. You didn't notice them because they're so small and quiet."

"Don't they do what you do?" I asked.

"They massage the legs and keep the blood flowing," the guy said, "but they don't move the ankles and knees and the hips."

That made sense.

"There's really no substitute for manual treatments," the guy said. "Plus, while I'm here, I check for potential pressure sores or bruises."

"I thought the nurses look for bed sores," I said.

"Everyone looks," he said. "It's what we fear most in long-term coma, but…"

He stopped. I'll bet he wasn't supposed to talk that way to "The Family."

"We all keep a sharp lookout for pressure sores, and you've probably noticed that we move your dad often, so that his weight is supported differently during the day."

I nodded.

The guy moved around the bed and worked on Dad's left arm for a few minutes.

"Would you like to help me with the stockings?" he asked.

"Sure," I said. "I need to learn this stuff."

I held Dad's left leg while he slipped on the left stocking, and he held Dad's right leg while I slipped on the other stocking. Then he showed me how to hook up the hoses and flip the *ON* switch, then make sure everything was working OK. Air flowed in and out of the bags around Dad's legs, squeezing and unsqueezing his calves. It looked like it felt pretty good.

"Those would be good after soccer practice," I said.

The guy smiled. "Professional athletes use them when they fly long distances right after a game," he said. "It helps the muscles heal much quicker, especially the old guys."

"Cool," I said. I'd have to see if I could get a set for me.

The guy made some notes in the computer and had one last look around the room.

"Good night, Isaac," he said.

Chapter 20:
No Cure-All.

"You must be tired of airports," I said, sliding a bowl of oatmeal to Uncle Bob.

He nodded his head, just a little, and spooned some brown sugar into his bowl.

He pointed at the milk, which I slid to him, and he splashed some over the sugar.

Then it was quiet.

"Would you gentlemen like some eggs?" Mom said as she walked into the kitchen. She was more awake than Uncle Bob and me put together.

Uncle Bob just pointed at his bowl.

"No, thanks," I said.

Mom smiled and put the frying pan away.

"Do you want oatmeal?" I asked.

Mom smiled. "No, Isaac, thank you, though. Just toast and coffee."

She put a little butter and a smear of jam on her toast and slid under the table across from Uncle Bob.

"Isaac is the new varsity goalie," she said, smiling.

Uncle Bob looked up from his bowl and opened his eyes a little.

"Shocking, huh?" I said.

"Not shocking," Uncle Bob said, "just unlikely. Not too many freshmen make varsity, especially at goalie. There's too much experience required at that position."

"I had to break the real goalie," I said, "to clear a spot."

Mom thought that was pretty funny, but I had to explain about the distracting talking and the broken hand before Uncle Bob saw the humor.

"Still, though," he said, "goalie is pretty tough. You'll probably not going to have much fun while you really learn the position."

"I'll be fine," I said. "I'm already bigger and faster than Caleb, the old goalie."

"You'll be OK," Uncle Bob said, "but you'll get beat a few times while you learn. Don't let it get you down."

Not too encouraging. It was quiet while Mom got herself another coffee.

"I had a long talk with Mrs. Morgan," I said when Mom got back to the table.

"That's great," Mom said. "What did you talk about?"

"She said that she used to just sit and talk with her husband, while he was dying. She was almost happy about it."

Mom squeezed her coffee cup, and the corners of her eyes crinkled up.

"What?" I said. I didn't think that would be a bad thing to say.

Mom just looked at her coffee. Her knuckles were white.

"He had a stroke?" Uncle Bob asked. "I don't really remember."

Mom nodded. "Right after we moved here."

She took a sip of her coffee, but I think it was still too hot.

"It was a very bad stroke," she said. "They had to withhold treatment."

Mom looked terrible. I was afraid to say anything else. It was quiet for a long, long time.

"I need to go," Mom said finally.

I came out of my room at lunchtime. Uncle Bob was making ham sandwiches.

"I guess I made Mom sad," I said.

He looked at me, then went back to spreading butter on the bread.

"No," he said. "Or yes. Probably. There's lots of ways things can go bad. It's hard to know what you can and can't say."

He put some ham slices on the buttered bread, then added some clean bread, then tossed one on a plate for me. He picked up the other one and took a bite. A big bite.

"What did she mean," I said, taking the plate, "that Mrs. Morgan had to withhold treatment?"

Uncle Bob chewed for a while, then swallowed.

"It used to be…" he said. Then he stopped. "A long time ago, people died all the time for all kinds of reasons. Usually nobody knew why exactly. You could die from an infected zit, or from an allergic reaction to a bee sting, or from eating the wrong foods, or not eating the right foods…"

"Like scurvy," I said. "You need limes."

"Exactly," Uncle Bob said, "lots of people died from lack of vitamin C."

I took a bite of my sandwich.

"Anyway, doctors got better and better at treating disease, so fewer and fewer people died for simple reasons."

"But you can't fix everything," I said.

"Right. We can't fix everything. So people still die."

I just waited.

"Everybody dies," I said. "Life is fatal."

Uncle Bob just looked at me for an hour or so.

"But what happens now," Uncle Bob continued finally, "is that sometimes we can fix part of what's wrong but not other parts. For instance, if someone has a spinal injury, if they break their back, maybe we can repair the bone damage, but we can't repair the nerve damage."

"So people are paralyzed." I said.

"Yeah," he said, "and some people really, really hate being paralyzed."

"And they wish they were dead," I said. I'd read a book about that once.

"And they wish they were dead," Uncle Bob said. "But usually people learn to adapt to physical disabilities and eventually live productive lives."

I just waited.

"But sometimes…" Uncle Bob said, and then he stopped. I could tell he was getting to the hard part.

"Sometimes, we deal with very severe injuries where it's not at all clear how we should proceed. This is especially common with traumatic brain injuries and stroke."

"Like Dad," I said.

"Let's start with Mr. Morgan," he said. "He had a very severe stroke, which means bleeding into the brain, and it destroyed his ability to communicate with and experience the world. His body was fine, and his doctors could keep his body alive for a very long time, but his mind was gone."

"So they killed his body," I said.

"So they let his body die. They made him comfortable, kept him sedated, and out of pain, and they stopped feeding him."

I shrugged. Seemed like the same thing.

"It can be very, very difficult for the people involved," Uncle Bob said. He looked right at me. "Very difficult."

I looked back at him.

"Dad?"

He nodded a little and took a bite of his sandwich. Then he crossed his arms and leaned back against the counter.

"So today," he said, "we're going to start decreasing your father's sedation level. By tomorrow afternoon, we should have a good idea of how much brain function your dad has left. Over the next few days, we'll start putting together a plan to bring your dad back home and get his life back together."

"Unless…"

"Unless we can't," Uncle Bob said.

My hands didn't feel right, and they started to shake. The kitchen didn't look right, either. It was like the lights got brighter. Way brighter.

"Isaac?" Uncle Bob was yelling at me. He had bread crumbs in the corners of his mouth.

Chapter 21:
It Can Get Pretty Bad.

I was on the couch. I didn't have my sandwich.

Then Uncle Bob walked in from the kitchen. He had a plate in his hand.

"Is that my sandwich?" I asked.

He just smiled. "You better eat," he said. "It will help you feel better. Then we'll talk some more."

"Did I pass out?" I said, sitting up.

He just shrugged and handed the plate to me.

"I'll get you some water," he said.

"Maybe some juice," I said to his back.

"Maybe some water," he said.

I finished my sandwich and took a big drink of water.

"So what's going to happen?" I said.

Uncle Bob was sitting in Dad's chair.

"With your dad?" he asked.

I shrugged, then nodded.

"We don't know."

"Sure you do," I said. "You're a doctor."

Uncle Bob took a deep breath and rubbed his knees with his hands. "OK," he said, "we do know some things. We know that your dad's seizures are somewhat under control. The medicine we're using seems effective, and we should be able to keep the seizures small and infrequent while we titrate, or adjust, dosages."

"A seizure is like an electrical storm in his brain, right?" I asked. I'd been reading.

"Sure," he said, taking another breath. "OK. We also know the seizure medication will make your dad groggy and unresponsive, so we'll need to allow for that while we evaluate his condition."

"So we won't panic if he's dopey?" I said.

Uncle Bob just looked at me. "We'll assume that at least some grogginess and depressed mental capacity will be due to the medication, yes. Also, as time goes on, we should be able to reduce the medication levels, so his responsiveness should improve."

"He'll need help walking around?"

Uncle Bob rubbed his knees again. "You'll need some patience," he said. "We're going to need to start right at the beginning. Hopefully your dad will be able to chew and swallow for himself, so we can remove the feeding tube. Hopefully he'll be able to breathe on his own, so we can remove the respirator. It's likely he'll need help with both of those things, and physical therapy is often effective. Walking is pretty far away right now."

Dad might not ever walk?

"How bad can it be?" I asked.

Uncle Bob sat up real straight, then his shoulders collapsed. I already knew the answer.

"Pretty bad," he said. "As bad as it gets."

Chapter 22:
Clarity...

The next morning, I had breakfast with Mom and Uncle Bob, then they left to sit with Dad before the doctors tried to wake him up. I didn't want to spend the whole day there. Jimi called and wanted to come over, but I told him no.

Finally, after lunch, I decided to walk to the hospital. I called Mom and told her she didn't need to pick me up, and she said that I had a couple more hours before Dad would start waking up.

It was a sunny day for a walk, and I wasn't surprised to see Mrs. Morgan out working on her flowers. She was still wearing her church dress.

"It's a beautiful day, Mr. Farmer!" she called, clipping off a dead rose. You need to clip off the dead ones so the new ones will grow. She told me that a long time ago.

"Hello, Mrs. Morgan," I said. "Your flowers look great."

She smiled a huge smile and clipped off a perfect pink bud. "Please give this to your mother," she said, "and tell her that I'm thinking of her."

I took the flower. It smelled as pretty as it looked.

"You are headed to the hospital?" she said.

"Yes," I said, "Dad should come out of his coma today."

"Well," she said, "you better take a flower for him, too." She clipped off a yellow bloom and handed it to me.

I took the yellow flower and just stood there, with a flower in each hand.

"Mrs. Morgan…" I said.

"We need to do something with those stems," she said, "so they don't dry out on the way to the hospital."

I nodded.

"Let's go inside, then," she said, taking the flowers from me and walking into the house. Spoodle met us at the porch stairs, then ran ahead of us through the door.

In the kitchen, Mrs. Morgan wrapped each stem in a wet paper towel, then in a piece of aluminum foil. Spoodle was taking big slurpy drinks from his water dish. She handed the flowers to me, and I held them both in my left hand.

"That should do," she said.

"Mrs. Morgan," I started again.

"Yes, dear," she said, looking right at my eyes. I'll bet that hurt her neck.

"How did you know?"

"Know what?"

"About Mr. Morgan, about…"

"When to let him go?"

I looked at my feet. "Yeah," I said.

Mrs. Morgan stood up, as tall as she could, and put her hands on my forearm, right below where I was holding the flowers. "Mr. Morgan and I were as close as two people can be, but we never imagined that something like that could happen, so we had never talked about it. When he got hurt, when he had the stroke, it was horrible. I felt all alone in the whole world."

I thought she would be sad, but she was smiling.

"But I thought of our love for each other and how lucky he was to have someone he loved and trusted to help him, and I was sure he trusted me to make the right decision."

She was still smiling. She was telling me the most horrible story in the world, and she was smiling.

"So," she said, "when the decision had to be made, I made it."

I was crying. Pretty hard. Not blubbering or anything, but my eyes were dripping all over, and my nose was running. Spoodle would have to lick up the floor.

Mrs. Morgan was still smiling.

"Your mom loves your dad," she said. "That will be enough. Now go."

Chapter 23:
Because Life Is…

By the time I got to the hospital, the yellow flower was completely open, and the pink bud was loosening a little.

"They're beautiful!" Mom said. She and Uncle Bob were sitting on a bench, outside the front door of the hospital. Then she made a serious face. "Does Mrs. Morgan know you took them?"

"She…"

Mom was laughing.

"Nope," I said. "I had to sneak inside and steal the foil, too. Spoodle almost caught me."

Uncle Bob smiled and looked at his feet. Then he leaned back and stretched out, with his toes pointed and his arms extended behind his head. He tapped his toes together, twice, then sat straight again, with his hands meshed in his lap.

"No flowers for you, Uncle Bob," I said. "Sorry."

"I don't need flowers," Uncle Bob said, squinting up at me. "This sunshine is enough." He crossed his arms over his chest, closed his eyes, and leaned his head back. You could almost see his face warm up.

"You guys are happy," I said. "Dad must be good!"

Mom smiled down into her flowers and smelled the yellow one. "We don't know," she said. "We still don't know."

Then she smiled up at me. Uncle Bob didn't move.

"I thought…"

"In an hour," Mom said. "The doctor said to check back in an hour"—she checked her watch—"fifteen minutes ago. So in forty-five minutes. Dad's not responding as quickly as they thought he would."

"So that's bad," I said. "Why…"

"It's not bad," Uncle Bob said. He didn't move, but he talked. Maybe his mouth moved. I didn't see it.

"It's not good," I said.

This time, Uncle Bob opened his eyes. "It's not good; it's not bad. It's just slower than they thought. It's just what it is. That's where we're at now. It just is what it is."

I sat next to Mom. There wasn't a lot of room on the bench, but Mom didn't slide over, so our shoulders were touching. I guess she didn't want to crowd into Uncle Bob. I guess it wasn't so bad that our shoulders touched.

I crossed my hands in my lap and leaned back, with my eyes closed. The sun did feel good.

"No good, no bad?" I asked.

"Right," Uncle Bob said.

"Just what is," Mom said. "Just reality. That's enough for now."

"That's what Mrs. Morgan said."

Mom leaned into me a little. "What did Mrs. Morgan say?"

"Mrs. Morgan said that you love Dad," I said. "She said that would be enough."

I felt Uncle Bob put his hand on my shoulder, so I sat up and opened my eyes. Mom reached over and slid her hand between mine, finally meshing her fingers and squeezing my hand.

We just sat there, holding each other. The sun felt good. It was enough.

END

About the Author

Phil Rink is an author, professional mechanical engineer, inventor and entrepreneur, a licensed ship's captain, and a private pilot, and he has run science fairs and coached kids for years in sports (mostly soccer) and Science Olympiad teams.

Please review Jimi & Isaac books.
Spread the word. Help others find books they'll enjoy.

Read our other Jimi & Isaac Books!
Jimi & Isaac 1a: School Soccer
Jimi & Isaac 2a: Keystone Species
Jimi & Isaac 3a: Mars Mission
Jimi & Isaac 4a: Solar Powered

Be a FAN:
www.facebook.com/Jimi.Isaac.Books